MARGRET & H.A.REY'S

Curious George

and the Dump Truck

Illustrated in the style of H. A. Rey by Vipah Interactive

Houghton Mifflin Company   Boston

Copyright © 1999 by Houghton Mifflin Company

Based on the character of Curious George®, created by Margret and H. A. Rey.
Illustrated by Vipah Interactive, Wellesley, Massachusetts: C. Becker, D. Fakkel, M. Jensen,
S. SanGiacomo, C. Yu.

The text of this book is set in Adobe Garamond.
The illustrations are watercolor and charcoal pencil, reproduced in full color.

Library of Congress Cataloging-in-Publication Data

Curious George and the dump truck / illustrated in the style of H. A. Rey by Vipah Interactive.
p. cm.
Based on the original character by Margret and H. A. Rey.
Summary: Curious George creates a mess when he boards a dump truck and spills a load of dirt
in a pond but redeems himself when the dirt creates an island for ducks in the pond.
RNF ISBN 0-395-97832-7 PAP ISBN ISBN 0-395-97836-X PABRD ISBN 0-395-97844-0
[1. Monkeys — Fiction.   2. Dump trucks — Fiction.   3. Ducks — Fiction.]   I. Rey, Margret.
II. Rey, H. A. (Hans Augusto), 1898–1977.   III. Vipah Interactive.   IV. Title: Margret and H.
A. Rey's Curious George and the dump truck.   V. Title: Curious George and the dump truck.
PZ7.M33583   1999
[E] — dc21   99-31533
                                                             CIP AC

Manufactured in China

This is George.
He lived with his friend, the man with the yellow hat.
He was a good little monkey and always very curious.
This morning George was playing with his toys when he heard a funny noise outside his window.

It sounded like a QUACK.
George was curious. What could be
quacking underneath his window?

It was a duck, of course!
Then George heard another QUACK — and another.

Why, it was not just one duck — it was a mother duck and five small ducklings.

Ducklings were something new to George. How funny they were!

He watched the ducklings waddle after their mother. Where were they going?

George was not curious for long...

Soon he was waddling
after Mother Duck, too!

Now he could see where
they were going.

The ducks waddled all the way to the park. George loved the park. Today he saw children flying kites and gardeners planting trees by the pond. Then George saw something he had never seen in the park before.

It was a dump truck. And it was *big*—in fact, George was not even as tall as one wheel!

George forgot all about the ducklings and stopped to look.

It would be fun to sit in such
a big truck, thought George.

No one was inside the truck.
And the window was wide open.
George could not resist.

But sitting in a big
truck was not so fun for
a little monkey after all.

George could not even
see out the window.

He was too small.
If only there were something
to climb on.

Would this make a good step
for a monkey?

It did! Now George could see out the window. He saw grass and trees and a family eating a picnic. Suddenly George heard a low rumbling sound. Was it his stomach rumbling? he wondered. (It had been a long time since breakfast.)

But the rumbling was not coming from George's stomach...

It was coming from the back of the truck! George was curious. He climbed out of the window. Then, like only a monkey can, he swung

up to the top of the truck.
Now he could take a look.
He saw the truck was filled
with dirt.

George was excited.
What could be better than
a truck full of dirt?

George jumped right in the
middle of it. Sitting on top of
the dirt, George felt the truck
bed begin to tilt . . .

It tilted higher and higher. The dirt began to slide. It was sliding right into the pond—and George slid with it. George was having fun.

But the pile in the pond got bigger

and bigger

and BIGGER.

And soon the fun was gone.

Just then the gardeners came back from lunch and stood with their mouths wide open.

They saw the empty dump truck, the pile of dirt in the pond, and a very muddy monkey.

They knew just what had happened.

But before they could say a word, George heard a familiar sound.

He heard more quacking.
The gardeners heard it, too.
Then they heard people laughing.
  "Look!" said a girl. "The ducks
have their own island!"

Indeed they did. The pile of dirt made an island in the pond — and Mother Duck and all her ducklings were waddling right on top.

George was sorry he had made such a mess, but the gardeners didn't seem to mind. "We were planting more trees and flowers to make the park nicer for people," said one of the gardeners. "But you've made the park nicer for ducks, too."

Later a small crowd gathered at the pond. "Would you like to help me feed the ducks?" a girl asked George. George was delighted. Soon everyone was enjoying the park more than ever before, including the ducks, who were the happiest of all in their new home.

The end